How many have you read?

Two years on:

Sleep over

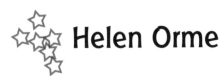 Helen Orme

Ransom

Sleepover

by Helen Orme
Illustrated by Chris Askham

Published by Ransom Publishing Ltd.
Radley House, 8 St. Cross Road, Winchester, Hampshire
SO23 9HX
www.ransom.co.uk

ISBN   978 184167 741 5

First published in 2011
Copyright © 2011 Ransom Publishing Ltd.

Illustrations copyright © 2011 Chris Askham

Meet the Sisters ...

Siti and her friends are really close. So close she calls them her Sisters. They've been mates for ever, and most of the time they are closer than her real family.

Siti is the leader – the one who always knows what to do – but Kelly, Lu, Donna and Rachel have their own lives to lead as well.

Still, there's no one you can talk to, no one you can rely on, like your best mates. Right?

1

Friday night

Lu was looking forward to Friday night.

'What time can they come?' she asked her mum.

'About six,' said Mum. 'Dad will be home by then and we can get the barbecue going.'

Lu arrived at school early. She couldn't wait to see the Sisters. They were her closest friends.

Siti was early too. She and Lu were talking about the sleepover when the others arrived.

'What are we going to eat?' asked Siti.

'Burgers, sausages and I've got some veggie stuff for Kelly,' said Lu. 'Mum's going to do some of her special rice and we've got loads of salads.'

Kelly had just decided that she didn't want to eat meat any more. She kept going on about how much she liked animals.

'I've got a great DVD,' said Kelly. 'I've borrowed it from Jamie. It's really, really scary.'

'We'll have to watch it in my bedroom then,' said Lu. 'You know what my mum's like about horror movies!'

2

Camping out

They got to Lu's house early. The barbecue was great. Lu's dad did all the cooking. He always took over any barbecue.

While he was cooking they went to get their beds sorted out. They weren't sleeping indoors. Lu's mum thought they would have more fun if they camped out in the summer house.

Lu's house was quite big, with a huge garden. The summer house was right at the bottom.

'You'll be out of the way down here,' said Lu's mum. 'I know what you lot are like – you'll be talking most of the night and I don't want to be kept awake. We're off to see Po-po and Gong-gong early tomorrow morning.'

'Give them my love,' said Lu. 'Tell them I'll come next time.'

'Who?' asked Siti.

'My grandparents,' explained Lu. 'We always call them that. It's what they say in Chinese.'

'Now, come on,' said Lu's mum. 'Let's get started or Dad will have cooked all the food before we've finished.'

They cleared most of the furniture out of the summer house and fitted in the loungers as beds.

'This would make a great house,' said Donna.

'But there's no water,' said Siti. 'That could make things a bit difficult!'

Lu's mum laughed. 'That reminds me,' she said 'We'll leave the patio door unlocked in case you need the bathroom, but don't make a lot of noise if you come in.'

3

Looking spooky

The food was really good and they were all stuffed.

'We're going to go up to my room now,' said Lu. 'We'll go down to the summer house about 10.30. Is that O.K.?'

'Fine,' said her mum. 'Just remember what I said about noise.'

'We'll be really quiet,' promised Lu. 'You won't even know we're here.'

'I'll leave everything ready for breakfast,' said her mum. 'We'll be gone before you get up.'

'Thank you for everything,' said Siti. 'I'll make sure everyone behaves!'

Donna hit her on the arm. 'You sound just like your dad,' she said. 'Are you practising to be a teacher too?'

Siti laughed. 'Just being polite,' she said.

They settled down to watch Kelly's DVD. It was about a group of people locked in a very old house. All sorts of monsters were hiding and whenever anyone went off on their own they got grabbed. It really was scary.

When it ended they got their gear and went outside. Because it was summer it was still sort of light. But it was the sort of light that made everything look spooky.

They ran down to the summerhouse.

'Have any of you ever seen a ghost?' asked Lu.

'My mum said she heard footsteps in an old house when there was no one there,' said Donna.

'Don't let's talk about ghosts,' begged Rachel.

But it was too late – they were all thinking about creepy things.

It was ages before they got to sleep.

4

Heavy breathing!

Of course, it was Rachel who heard it first. She sat up with a start. A screeching noise came from somewhere close by.

Her heart was pounding and her mouth was dry. She listened. She could hear a strange puffing noise.

She reached over to Siti, who was sleeping next to her.

'Quick, wake up,' she hissed. 'There's someone outside. He's doing heavy breathing!'

'What? What's going on?' Siti sat up too. She banged her head on something and shrieked loudly.

'Shut up!'

'What's going on?'

'What's the matter?'

Now everyone was awake.

'There's someone out there – I can hear him!'

Lu switched on the light. She opened the door.

'Don't do that – he'll get you.' Rachel tried to grab Lu.

Kelly put on a torch. She shone it outside.

'Look, that's your 'someone!"

It was a hedgehog!

They all went out.

'Look, he's sweet really,' said Lu. 'We always put out food for him in the summer. That's why he's here. I could have told you what the noise was if you hadn't made so much fuss.'

Rachel got cross. 'Well I didn't know, did I?' she snapped.

'Come on,' said Siti. 'Back to bed.'

5

It might come back!

But before they could shut the door something even more scary happened.

A black thing swooped down in front of them.

This time it was Donna who screamed.

A light went on in the house. Bedroom curtains were pulled open. Then there really

was someone in the garden. It was Lu's
mum.

'What on earth are you doing?' She
sounded really cross. 'You know we have to
get up early.'

'Sorry, mum,' said Lu. 'There was a scream, then it was the hedgehogs, then there was a bat.'

'Go back to bed,' said her mum. 'No more noise or you'll all have to come indoors.'

They went back inside. Donna shut the
door firmly.

'But what was that scream?' asked Rachel. 'It was really scary.'

'It was either a fox or an owl.' said Lu. 'They both make a loud noise.'

'I don't care what it was,' said Kelly. 'Let's get back to bed.'

'But what about that bat thing?' said Donna. 'It might come back.'

'Well it can't get in can it?' said Siti. 'We've shut the door.'

'It's too hot in here,' complained Kelly.

Lu opened the window. 'O.K. now?'

They settled down. Rachel decided whatever noises she heard for the rest of the night, she wasn't going to take any notice at all.

 27

The next time it was Kelly who screamed. She was woken by something heavy landing on her tummy.

6

Get out of here!

'It's all right,' mumbled Lu, 'It's only the cat.'

But it wasn't all right!

Siti flashed the torch. It was the cat, but it was something else as well. The something was hanging from its mouth.

'It's got a rat!'

Then it got even worse. The cat dropped the rat. He wanted to play games with it. The rat made a dash under Kelly's bed. She screamed again.

The cat was jumping all over them trying to catch the rat again.

'Quick, we've got to get out of here!' Lu yanked the door open.

The Sisters got out as fast as they could.
Lu slammed the door.

'What are we going to do now?' asked
Donna. 'We can't go back in there with the
rat.'

'We'll have to go indoors,' said Lu. 'But
we'll have to be really quiet. If we wake
Mum again, she'll kill us.'

They went back up the garden. The cat decided they were going to play and jumped out of the window to follow them. He wound himself round Siti's feet and she nearly fell over. Then he ran off.

'Thank goodness,' thought Siti. 'Maybe it'll go and kill that rat.'

But the cat didn't head back to the summer house. Instead it ran up the garden and jumped up on the car.

'So much for being quiet!' said Rachel. The outside light had come on and the car started hooting to itself.

'That stupid cat!' exclaimed Lu.

It took ages to sort it all out. Lu's dad stopped the car alarm and then went off to deal with the rat.

The sisters sat in the kitchen and tried to explain to Lu's mum just why it really wasn't their fault.

'There was no need to fuss,' said Lu's dad. 'It wasn't a rat, just a mouse. I've taken it out to the front garden.'

'But that's just as bad as a rat,' said Kelly.

'I thought you liked animals,' said Donna.

'I do. But not jumping all over me in the middle of the night.'

It was nearly 3 o'clock by the time they were all settled again.

1

Time to get up

At six o'clock, Lu's mum crept in. She poked Lu gently.

'We're off now,' she whispered. 'I've locked the door. Here's the key.'

Lu took the key.

'Bye,' she said sleepily.

When she woke again the sun was very bright. She could hear footsteps. She heard a voice. Two voices.

She got up and peeped out of the window. There were Siti's dad and Kelly's mum.

Kelly's mum knocked on the summer house door. Lu got up and opened it.

Kelly's mum looked at the sleepy girls.

'Well,' she said. 'You look as if you had a good time.'

'Come on,' called Siti's dad. 'Time to get up, you lazy lot.'

'Come back later,' said Siti. 'I need a little nap!'